THE SPACE KID 2- ESCAPE ELECTRO MAGNETIC FIELDS

VARAD KALE

ISBN 979-888555670-5

The Space Kid 2

Contents

Acknowledgements

Varad Kale with Padma Bhushan Sri Dr. Vijay Bhatkar

CHAPTER ONE

A New Day

Monday, 31ˢᵗ December, 3021

Today I've completed all my detentions and litter duties, and I felt pretty relaxed.

And yes, I am Erick woods, a student in APJ high, a tech-kid who lives in the year 3021.

The last week was bad, as I spent it in detention, and the week before, me and my friends were fighting aliens who were invading our ship. WE WON, after sending them on a frozen planet.

And hey, do you know there's a new principal in the school named Steward Woods (Matching last name is just a coincidence, he is not my relative)? If you didn't, now you know.

When I entered the school today, I felt my popularity fading, and I was REALLY happy about it, as I don't like fans' (kids') crowd gathered around me.

"Hi Erick!" Rodrick cried out.

"Hey, Whaddup?" I asked.

He told me that there's a new class, in which we will be taught to fly spaceships. I thought he was joking and ignored him, as I know he likes joking.

CHAPTER TWO

First Period

Monday, 31ˢᵗ December, 3021

You know, the thing Rodrick was telling was true, we were in a room full of spaceships (small ones, made for only one person).

"Kids, get into your spacecraft!" Our teacher thundered.

I quickly got into the spacecraft with my name, but I was very unfamiliar with the controls.

I could see a power switch and turned it on, and my spacecraft's engine started ROARING.

"Kids, now switch the speed controls on, and put the speed to hundred, and remember students, my name is Vincent." Our flight teacher, Vincent ordered.

I didn't even know which were the controls I was supposed to put on hundred, that's when I noticed something, there was a blue hologram around one joystick. I supposed it was the speed control, but still, I didn't know how much I must move the lever to get hundred. I still pulled the lever, and a display in front of me flickered to life, and it was showing some complex diagrams and the number '0'. As I pushed the lever, the number increased and when I pulled it, the number decreased. I quickly switched it to hundred, and the engines' roaring got louder.

That's when the ceiling opened, and I could see the space above me. I wasn't in a room; it was a HANGER DECK.

"Students, now turn on the voice controls, and speak 'start', and remember to steer!" Vincent commanded.

A button was now covered in hologram, and I switched it on.

"Start." I spoke.

At that instant, two things happened.

- The spacecraft started moving forward
- There was a holo-ring in my left hand, which I supposed the steering controls

The spacecraft was speeding up and was gonna crash straight on an asteroid as we were practicing in the open space.

I processed an unknown algorithm in my brain and found that the thingy in my left hand was the ring version of the spacecraft in which I was sitting. I turned the ring towards the right, and the ship turned towards right.

"EASY!!" I shouted.

The moment I completed saying it, the spacecraft's language changed from English to **Gibberish** (with 'Gibberish', I meant unknown symbols) and the spacecraft started trembling.

I hit the SOS button, but the response too was in Gibberish (this time, with 'Gibberish', I meant unknown words).

The ring in my hand started vanishing and the spacecraft started going out of my control, and it all ended up with a huge crash. Good that the spacecraft's safety system was working, or else I would've been a scrambled egg till now.

"How was your FIRST flight Erick" Rodrick cried out with a grin.

"Wow... it was really awesome." I replied sarcastically.

I saw a spacecraft landing gracefully on the floor and was surprised to see BEATRICE coming out of the spacecraft!

I replaced a confused look with Rodrick, and we both started marching towards her.

"Hi guys, I learnt pretty good flying today." Beatrice said.

"That was fantastic!" Rodrick said, impressed by her skills.

"Children!" Vincent BOOMED, looking at US!!!!

"What's the matter with ye? Why talking in the class..." he started "And why did you crash, Idiot" He said, pointing towards ME!!!

I told him that the spacecraft I was flying was speaking and displaying Gibberish. He was shocked at what I said.

He had a look at my spacecraft, and gave me one-day detention, as my spacecraft was looking all right.

I was feeling VERY bad as I was getting detention at the NEW year's eve.

CHAPTER THREE

THE SHOCKING NEWS

Monday, 31st December, 3021

You know, I was feeling very nice today after school as my detention was finished.

After the school ended, I got my holographic pen out and got a SHOCKING NEWS!

Last week, when people heard that I, Beatrice and Rodrick defeated some ALIENS who were invading our school's spaceship, there were many investigations by space-police, and they found out that there are many developed alien civilizations in our neighboring planets.

The next thing happened was, HUMANS made an alien translator, which can detect the feelings behind the aliens' languages' sound waves and convert them in English.

Scientists, astronomers and political leaders communicated with the aliens and formed a combined civilization and named it as nebula.

New laws were made, and now aliens can come to earth for education and humans can go to other planets (it happened that fast cuz the pre-made arrangements in case we *did* find alien civilizations).

BUT!! There's the bad news, aliens were gonna come to our school, the APJ school from the New Year's Day, i.e., TOMMOROW!!!!!!!!

THERE WOULD BE ANOTHER INVASION!

I quickly reached Beatrice and Rodrick to tell them the news I had, and when I told them about the invasion, they started laughing like IDIOTS.

"Guys, seriously, there's no time to laugh, we have got a school to save." I said.

"Quit JOKING" Beatrice said

"Yeah, that's too much Erick... he hee..." Rodrick said while laughing.

Were my friends really mad?

"I'm not joking!" I screamed at the top of my lungs.

"Hey Erick, let's get one thing straight- it sounds like a joke when you say it, and if you are serious, let me tell you that the aliens will be surrounded by galactic laws, and they'll be KIDS! I think I can learn pretty awesome things from them." Beatrice said.

At her words, I was a comforted, but a part of me was sure that they'll invade us!

CHAPTER FOUR

PARTYYYYY!!!

Monday, 31ˢᵗ December, 3021

At the night, a GREAT surprise was waiting for me, Rodrick decided to invite me and Beatrice for a grand dinner, he had arranged with his last three months' pocket money.

I quickly got a hoverboard outta the basement and zoomed off.

When I was at the most expensive and the GRANDEST restaurant.

"Hi Erick, do you know where Beatrice is?" Rodrick asked.

"Hey, let's visit here mansion, I think she'll be inventing something new... it's her old behavior. BTW, I was thinking this for a long time, can I call you Rod, instead of Rodrick?" I replied.

With a nod, Rodrick started running towards Beatrice's mansion, and I followed him.

Huff... Puff... it was a long journey; her mansion was quite far.

When we reached there, her mansion was

GLOWING YELLOW. I was feeling a bit afraid, as sometimes her experiments are dangerous, the last time I remember, Beatrice was experimenting with some chemicals found on planet zeta-b-2 (yeah, this is just a code, the planet isn't inhabited, hence doesn't have a name), her bedroom was just a pile of ash, luckily, got it repaired before anyone knew.

"Y- you'll g- go first" Rodrick said, hesitating.

"N- no... you-" I said.

"K, we'll knock together." Rodrick Rod said.

We moved our hands to knock at the door, but when we touched the door's surface, there was a loud BOOM!

I jumped till the roof of our spaceship... okay, it wasn't a mile high, but you get the picture...

When I was down, I saw Beatrice glaring at me from the window.

"Hey guys, 'sup?" Beatrice asked us, she was looking a little roasted.

"Sick dude, didn't have a bath since a week?" I asked.

"It was just an explosion." Beatrice replied

I took a sigh of relief, Rodrick did the same, if we would've arrived a little early, we would've been a victim of the explosion!!

Beatrice showed us her latest invention, it was an alien communicator!!

I gasped after looking at it.

It was named 'alien communicator' but it was a room-sized space shuttle, equipped with practically EVERYTHING!!!!

"Guys, what are we waiting for? It's time to fly!!" Beatrice squealed with excitement in her voice.

We quickly dived in, and the entrance closed with a hissing sound until it seemed like there wasn't any door at all.

"Hey Beatrice, beat some rice, but to fly in the space, we'll have to break the roof!" I told Beatrice.

"No Worries Erick, I've beat the rice just now, and this thing has built-in teleporters!" Beatrice said.

That thing is simply insane, teleporters are very cool, and very rare in 3021!!!!

She pressed a button, and the ship started hovering above the floor.

"GX-ULTRA, teleport us outside." Beatrice said.

No way! GX-ULTRA was my AI and invention, I invented it to defeat aliens, but while upgrading it, Beatrice and Rodrick BROKE the hardware and copied the system into my holographic pen... and secretly they copied it in their holo-pen.

I misplaced my pen with GX-ULTRA, and Beatrice kept using it...

"Hey Beatrice! You can't use my invention in your invention!" I protested.

"Calm down Erick, it'll help you." GX-ULTRA said in the calmest voice I could think of.

I don't know what happened, but I immediately calmed down.

As soon as the 'Alien Communicator' started the teleportation process, I felt like each atom of my body got separated and re-assembled after getting to a new place!!

Now, the only thing I could see was space.

"eh?" Rodrick ASKED, confused.

"You are too ancient to understand, Rodrick..." Beatrice started "This is the teleportation technology, which separates all your atoms and reassembles them on a new place." Beatrice finished.

"You know, if we're lucky, we can see *The Ancient Dragons of The Space,* the dragon clan which migrates from solar system-to-solar system in search of a new home, they are really big! The babies are half a mile loooooooong!!"

Beatrice explained.

I was surprised at the fact she told.

We zoomed towards the end of the Galaxy, in which our school was... you know, we couldn't reach the end as the 'alien communicator' wasn't that fast.

BUT!!! The worse thing happened next. When we got back to the place our school was SUPPOSED to be, there wasn't anything!

I remembered that there was rumor that the ship was moving thirty times the speed of light around the galaxy to avoid any possible dangers and maintaining universal balance by a secret device! If that was true, till now our school would've reached in a different galaxy!!!!

The next thing was the worst, our teleporter EXPLODED 'cause of overload, which meant that we couldn't teleport anymore!

I explained my friends 'bout the rumor, which gave Rodrick a heart-attack... okay, it wasn't a REAL attack, but you'll get the picture.

Beatrice opened the teleportation system, and found it wasn't completely destroyed... we replaced some of the parts with junk that we could get, the best that we could do at this time. After a lot of effort, we assembled the whole teleporter and calculated the position of Beatrice's mansion and teleported there, phew! WE WERE SAFE, WOO, HOOOO!!

We continued our new-year party and now, I'm writing my journal.

I am very sleepy and its almost 3 in the morning, we were partying till 2 AM, and I am very sleepy right now, so byeeeeeee...

This isn't THAT bad

CHAPTER-5 'This isn't THAT bad'

Tuesday, 1st January, 3022

Okay, let me admit that today's day wasn't that bad, but yeah, the aliens were very different than us.

Today when I woke up, I got a news that school had announced a holiday because today we were supposed to interact and be friends with the aliens.

When I got out of my bed, the first thing I did was, got to the **TARTARUS** and found some leftover taser guns which we made to fight the aliens a week back, they weren't aloud, but the aliens were stealing our ship, so we had to break some tiny school rules, sorry to the god...

When I got the guns, I grabbed my hoverboard and raced till the lab on my 4th floor.

In the lab, I got some energy sources like unzite planotomia, virzikites, grinzigate, etc. those energy sources are all called mineralals as a group. I fixed them into my hoverboard. The mineralals would boost the speed of my hoverboard so that I could get away if the aliens were chasing me. After a LOT of other preparations, I was ready to roam free.

- I added the mineralals to my hoverboard.

- I equipped it with pepper spray and other irritational things like that.
- I got my old one-time-use taser gun and made it unlimited-shooter!
- I got a translator.
- I practiced flying spacecrafts, in case I had to abandon the school and the spaceship.

Phew... it was pretty sick preparation for an alien attack.

I was really SHOCKED to see aliens as KIDS, they were all in different shapes and sizes, some of them had hands, tentacles, antennas, fins and other things which I hadn't seen at all!!

"Slurpsjuiuyghasbguy." An alien said looking towards me, excited.

I thought he was gonna ambush me!! I quickly put the mineralals of speed on my hoverboard and got out of his reach.

"Huff..." I took a sigh of relief.

I was thinking about the thing that alien said, then I remembered 'bout the TRANSLATOR, which reads the emotions behind the soundwaves and all...

When I was hoverboarding towards the restaurant when someone KNOCKED me down, with my head beating on the concrete road! I'd expected to see HEAVEN's beauty, but I saw Beatrice!

"What is this, Beatrice? You almost killed me! I think I have to pass a night, or maybe two at the Nebulae-Doctors!!" I shouted at Beatrice

Do you know who are the Nebulae-Doctors? If not, they are our school's Doctors, who NAIL their work with the most advance hospitalization and robots.

Anyway, Beatrice was laughing loudly!

"How was it? NERD! I know you thought it was an alien-attack, now, get up, and let's eat something, Rodrick's also here" Beatrice teased me.

As we were walking down the road to 'Grab n Go', we saw very different types of aliens, which caused my skin to almost escape from my body, you get the picture, right?

"I am also an ALIEN, and I'll KILL ya humans" Rodrick said, teasing me.

"Hey both of you! Stop teasing me!" I shouted

They both laughed at me, but I didn't feel bad, they're
My friends.

We grabbed some pizza and headed towards the cafeteria, and we were joking all the way.

"Knock." Said Beatrice

"Who's there?" Asked Rodrick

"Woo." Beatrice said excitedly

"Woo who?" Rodrick asked, feeling a little bored.

"Don't get too excited, it's just a joke." Beatrice said.

We all laughed at her funny joke.

Rodrick was next-

"Knock knock." Rodrick said

"Who's there?" Beatrice asked

"Boo." Rodrick said

"Boo who?" Beatrice asked, wondering what would come next "Oh, don't cry Beatrice, it's only a joke." We all had a good laugh, except for Beatrice, who was having the BEST laugh.

We, Rodrick and I, laughed louder looking at Beatrice.

The lunch was the same, we all were joking.

That's when Beatrice SHOUTED

"Today was the day!!!!"

"What happened." Rodrick and I asked her, it was looking like she had lost her marbles.

She explained that today interested students, including the aliens were supposed to volunteer in making an advance echo-system* for the ship, and she wanted to volunteer.

The PROBLEM was that the registration started at 10:30 AM, and ended at 1:45 PM, and when she told that, only one minute was left.

We all went into panic, that's when my brains flickered.

I had the mineralals of speed!!

"Hey Beatrice, grab my hoverboard and GO!! My hoverboard is equipped with bronenziteum, which is the mineralal of speed!" I shouted.

"Thanks, Eri—" Beatrice said, but as she took off, I couldn't hear the end of her sentence.

After a fraction of a second, Beatrice called me on my holographic pen.

"Hi Erick, I just got myself registered, thanks to you." She said, laughing.

"But using bronenziteum, you would take four seconds to reach there, and only half was passed when you called." I said, feeling confused.

"Bronenziteum is also used to teleport, and I knew the trick, and do you know that it can also time-travel? I think you don't" Beatrice said, which was absolutely and utterly true.

I was really excited at the fact she gave; I could use it if another alien invasion would happen, I could travel back in time, and bring the best warriors of all time to defeat those evil aliens.

When Beatrice was back, she explained her new project, for which she got herself registered.

She told that 'Advance eco-system' meant-

'Our school has an eco-system, but it is all artificial. It looks like nature, as we have a fake sun, fake plants, fake bushes, robo-bugs and all. The new project is that all the students must think a way, from which real plants could survive on our ship, for that we would need real sun and real insects! They all depend on one-another, so we have to manage all in a complicated manner.'

Huff... it was really complicated to do all that stuff, but Beatrice was looking interested.

But the worst thing was that I was supposed to HELP Beatrice, as she'd also registered me along with her!! Oh, poor MEEEEE!

The next day, we were starting.

The rest of the day, I was thinking ways to make a realistic sun, which would give real sunlight, then it HIT me, why MAKE an advance sun? We can settle our ship near a natural sun! But again, it hit me- we can't settle in a place, as we must drop each and every alien in their galaxies, and we can do it only if our traveling speed is speed of light x 30.

After it was the time for lights-off, I was searching for an inspiration, and was carving for cool ideas

So, good night as I am sleeping.

CHAPTER SIX

'I am just a kid! Not a laborer!!

Wednesday, 2ⁿᵈ January, 3022

Man, let me tell you a thing-

I am just a kid! Not a laborer!!

When I woke up, some dangerous-looking robots attacked me, they took me at the school, like I was their prisoner! There I saw the principal Steward, some kids, and one of them was BEATRICE!!

It was a trap set by the aliens! The aliens wanted to catch me, keep me as a servant and every HUMAN, including Beatrice were helping them... BEATRICE was a TRAITOR (I thought)!!!!

"You traitor!! How, how did I accept you as a friend, Beatrice! And even if I did, you and all the HUMANS, including our principal betrayed me!!" I shouted in front of everyone.

"No one is being betrayed. You registered yourself for the new eco project, and it's the time to start... we called at your mansion five time, but you didn't answer; so, we had to send those emotionless robots." Principal Steward said.

At his words, my cheeks turned red with embarrassment.

"According to the school rules, your statements' punishment would be three-day detention, BUT as you are volunteering for the eco project, you are safe." Steward exclaimed.

I took a sigh of relief.

When some kids were discussing their ideas, Beatrice came to me with a funny look on her face.

"Are you really nuts? How can I BETRAY you? Or are you really that big fool?" Beatrice teased me.

"Umm... I guess... I was being over-paranoid." I murmured softly.

"Good that you registered me here, or till now, I would've ended up in detention." I said to Beatrice.

"But if I hadn't, you won't be dragged over here, so you wouldn't have ended up in detention." Beatrice explained.

I am such a dumbo, I thought.

With a smile, she showed me the room, in which we were supposed to prepare awesome ideas.

I sat on an electro-magnetic chair, closed my eyes and started thinking.

I don't know how, but I dozed off...

"What??" I shouted when I was woken up by a LOUD voice.

"GET TO WORK, KID!!" a strange-looking robot shouted.

I quickly got to the desk and began scratching my notepad with some ideas I'd prepared last night.

"I SAID GET TO WORK!!!!" The robot shouted again.

"I am working, can't you see? Check-up your cameras." I shouted.

The robot pushed me out of the room, in the open.

"While you were sleeping, someone's idea was decided to be the final plan. I didn't like it, as it seems a little impractical." Beatrice explained.

She shown me the final plan's hologram.

"What rubbish!" I shouted looking at the hologram.

There were many wrong things in it-

1. It was useless.
2. mineralal of speed was used for conducting electricity, but instead of conducting electricity, the mineralal would destroy it.
3. Heavy materials were used, and the base was very small compared to the heavy materials.
4. Many other mineralals were put in wrong places.
5. If it was really made, it would fall, causing the destruction of the ship's server, because of which, the ship will stop working!!
6. It was supposed to make our old sun better than nature, but it would overload the sun, and it'll explode.
7. The design was basically a tower, which was a little underground. The position of the tower would be an obstacle for the ship's sewer system.
8. The tower needed more electricity than the entire SHIP!
9. The tower's electricity repulses would create a strong electro-magnetic field. The electro-magnetic field can cause major health diseases, and all the machines would EXPLODE.

We listed down each and every fault in the design and got more than THIRTY!!

"Hey, this design is really rubbish!" Beatrice shouted.

did I mention that Beatrice is the best in public-speaking? If not, now you know.

We showed the teachers the points we listed out, but they weren't even LOOKING at my notepad!

After all, nothing was left, and we had to work like the laborers who built the pyramid of Giza.

We huffed, puffed, lifted heavy thingies, fixed them in their place, got bruises, missed classes and more.

When I was working with the mineralals and electricity, an electricity panel EXPLODED!! Did I tell you that I was 10 feet above the floor? I started falling at blazing speed. I landed on a soft pillow they had placed on the ground, but it was a little thin, which made me CRY in pain.

The rest of the day was pretty uneventful, as I was on the bed at the Nebulae-Doctors.

Man, that was *really* close to death.

CHAPTER SEVEN

Good and Alive

Tuesday, 3rd January, 3022

Well, today I was alright and ready to work, which was really BAD, I don't wanna work like a laborer, I never did!!

I got out of the HOSPITAL early in the morning (8 AM) and found my mansion.

I slept there until a LOUD BOOMING noise woke me up.

"WHO!? WHAT!!?" I screamed.

"Hey there, fainting newbie." Rodrick shouted from out of the door.

If you don't know, 'fainting newbie' was my old nickname (I was fainted when I came to the school)

The BOOMING noise was nothing but the doorbell, and it wasn't even that loud as I heard it, alas I was snoring.

I invited Rodrick in, but he said we were already late for the school.

I spot a look on my Super-Smart watch, and found it was 9:15, and the school was gonna start in 5 MINUTES!!

I got my hoverboard and hit the road immediately.

I found some bronenziteum, and tried to figure out how to teleport, that's Beatrice stepped in.

"You're also late?" I asked.

"Not really, I was almost in the homeroom, when I saw your seats empty, I raced here as you two always find yourselves in some mess." She said.

She was a real friend, as 'A friend in need is a friend Indeed."

I asked Beatrice to help me teleport, and she just kicked the bronenziteum, and I found myself next to the school.

That's when I remembered that Rodrick wasn't there. I didn't want to get in the school, as Beatrice had helped me, so I couldn't go in the school without her.

I waited for my FRIENDS for a long time, but they weren't coming. Beaten-up, I got to my homeroom, that's when I found Beatrice and Rodrick SITTING there.

"I was waiting for you guys out, and you are sitting here!!" I shouted at them.

"I teleported you out there, and we teleported here, what's there to argue?!" Beatrice replied.

"I can't hold it anymore; it was a prank designed by Beatrice." Rodrick said laughing.

They both started laughing like idiots but stopped when a new teacher came to our class.

"Alien?" I shouted.

The new teacher had SIX hands and two tentacles coming from her back, plus she had FOUR legs and a furry body.

"Child, don't call me alien as I am your new homeroom teacher. You are thinking me as an alien as I am not an earthling, but according to galactic laws, I can be a teacher in APJ school." She said in a calm and sweet voice.

At the words 'Galactic laws', I calmed down a bit and sat in my place.

The homeroom was boring, and next came the FLIGHT class.

"Children! Get in your spacecrafts." Vincent Boomed.

I got in my spacecraft, and found a bully named 'Boloxinin' (not to judge or anything, but Boloxinin is a strange name) coming to hit me.

I came to know about him today, as he was also an alien inhabitant of a faraway planet (I stopped calling the alien as I realized it feels bad).

Rodrick told me that he randomly picked anyone who looked in his eyes, as on his planet named Pethagrononos, looking in one's eye meant 'Hey, I am better than you'.

I quickly remembered how to fly a spacecraft.

I switched the speed controls on, put them on 100, said 'start' and steered the ring in my hand.

I leapt with increasing confidence and was finally saved from that bully, as when he attacked me, I leapt sideward, which caused him crash in the wall. I quickly got out of the trouble, following Everyone in the vast space. Vincent had boomed some orders, but I didn't pay attention as I was being chased by Boloxinin.

It turned out that I SHOULD have listened the orders boomed by Vincent, as I was going away from our ship's gravitational field, and if I got out of the field, I would end up being 5588460 miles behind the ship in a second!!

I quickly turned the ship, and put the speed on thousand, when that didn't work, I started to worry a little (little more than the person who made a world-record of being worried). I used the last choice I had; I started the supersonic travel!

As the supersonic travel started, my mind stopped working, my one eyeball POPPED out of the bony socket, my right hand became a ball and started going away from the rest of my body, and I ended up ruining the whole shape and structure of my body!!

When the spacecraft ran out of supersonic energy, I gathered all my body parts, put them in their place and they self-assembled because of the leftover supersonic radiation.

I was surprised at the fact that I survived!!

I was really tired till the class was over, but still, Vincent said that I and Beatrice are the best pilots, and Rodrick can also catch-up. I was really happy that I could really fly a spacecraft!!

Next came the galactic history class. First, it was called *History* class, but after the aliens were here, they started teaching us history from all the inhabited planets around the cosmos; hence the name changed to *Galactic History*.

I got in the class, and just dozed off, as I was very sleepy because of the supersonic radiation. I just heard a thing in the whole class said by our teacher-

"King Beloxinoisedex of the planet 'Besudioxixinin' was expert in wars, he had over hundred thousand castles and over hundred billion square-kilometers of land. He just used one trick, he carried electro-magnetic weapons, and if the enemy did the same, he would produce a strong supersonic charge towards themselves to dodge the electromagnetic repulses.

This technique was used by him around three thousand years ago, when earth didn't know about machines.

Now, if you try the technique in a war, you'll be defeated as there are stronger weapons available, but this trick is useful if stuck in a place full of electromagnetic repulses and radiations."

Next came the science class.

As I got in the class, I was surprised that it was empty!

I searched the school for the people but couldn't find anyone. I looked in my holo-pen for any thermal signatures, and found only ONE trace, in the FLYING CLASS!

I got there and found everyone in my class in a spacecraft of their own.

"What's going on?!" I asked Beatrice.

"We are going to a field trip." Rodrick said.

"What's it about?" I again asked.

This time, Beatrice answered-

"Ms. Bethany is taking us to the Calsuset solar system in the Blasers galaxy, where we'll see all the planets lining up, this thing happens in each thousand YEARS!!!! We'll be the first people to see it as when it happened last time, people didn't even know it's happening, no planet in this universe had that strong technology to know!!"

I was really excited to see this thingy!!

I quickly ran towards Ms. Bethany.

"How are we gonna travel till the galaxy?" I asked the Ms. Bethany, she was not human, but almost looked human, she had a beautiful body like a human, and an elegant pair of wings on her back.

"This is not just a science-trip, but also a flying test. You will fly your own spacecraft WITHOUT any worries of bullies. The main school ship will fly ten miles behind you, but the ship would be invisible." Ms. Bethany said.

I was pretty excited for the test, and after all I was second-best pilot in our class.

We got some time to practice our skills, which was a DAY!! Now you might've been wondering why we got in the flying class in the first place, and the answer is- We needed to be informed about the bigger spacecrafts!

After Vincent was done telling us the controls of the bigger spacecraft (the controls were really the same as our smaller spacecrafts), we were told that we would be getting a training-area.

"Kids, get back in your mansions!" Vincent ordered.

WHAAAT, why getting in the mansions?? I was very angry.

When I was back in my mansion, the MAGIC happened, the phony sky (roof) opened, pushing all air in the space.

All the mansions were sealed to conserve the air inside them. I heard some noise in the basement. I was terrorized that there was a HOLE, which would suck all the air from my mansion, and I WOULD DIE!!!!!!

I quickly got to the basement and found that some barrels were loaded, which were filled with all sorts of non-toxic gases essential for the human body. The barrels looked long-lasting as they were made up of

Yr=10*peop=10*usa-ge (12328373) *, which means they could be used by ten people for a YEAR.

That's when all the speakers in my mansion BOOMED with Vincent's voice, which almost gave me a HEART-ATTACK!!

"Ha ha!" Vincent laughed "Tricked you children. Your mansions are now in space, like separate spaceships.

now your mansions will be getting some attachments to make them even BIGGER, and to expand them even more, your basements, first floors and second floors would be attached to the ground floors. And don't worry about your stuff, it will be teleported in the ship's 4D storage compartment" Vincent finally finished.

I don't want all my cool stuff (which probably wasn't allowed) going in the ship's 4D storage, I wanted to keep it with me! But that was also a problem as I had to practice flying entire SPACECRAFT in my mansion, then the lightbulb in my ? sparked. I had my own 4D storage, my bottomless bag!

Before my stuff was gone, I grabbed all the taser guns, video games, my hoverboard, all my mineralals and a lot of other stuff and put it in my bottomless bag. And finally, huff... my stuff was safe!!

I got my spacecraft coming towards my mansion, and I got inside.

I put the speed on hundred, started the ship and started steering it. I practiced taking off and landing for a while, which started to feel boring, that's when I got an idea, STUNTS!!!! I put the speed on five hundred and violently rotated the ring in my hand, I leapt then dived and then took a U-turn while my spacecraft's speed was on TWO THOUSAND!! I think you pretty much know how I ended up, so I don't want to tell you, as I ended up in brui_es...

I still practiced, as I don't want to get a 'C' in my first flight test.

At the end of the day, a spaceship came towards, and I called it a 'spaceship' instead of a 'spacecraft' as it was double the size of my mansion with the extension!

The spaceship stopped at my mansion.

"Hi Erick, you can come with us, we found some controls in our mansions, which converted them in spaceships. You can attach your mansion here too!" Beatrice said.

I assembled my mansion and we took turns controlling the SPACESHIP we had made.

I was tired till the end of the day, so I just separated my mansion and fixed it back on the main school-ship and slept tight.

CHAPTER EIGHT

The Trip

Tuesday, 3rd January, 3022

We were finally boarding to the Calsuset solar system!

I got my bottomless bag, wondering what it is like inside the bag... is it a black hole? I don't think so as I can fetch my stuff out anytime... was my stuff flying in zero g?

Anyway... I was going to my spacecraft when I met my friends, Beatrice and Rodrick.

We chatted till we reached the boarding station, where we got in our spacecrafts.

I gave the instructions, and took off...

It was pretty cool till we reached halfway, when something in my spacecraft EXPLODED!!! I was into full-panic mode, with all my palms sweaty, legs shaking and heavy breathing.

I remembered how to look for damaged parts using the holograms. I replaced the damaged communication system with a spare one, but till that time, everything was starting to explode!

I heard Vincent YELLING something over the speaker, but I was too horrified to pay attention, but it turns out I SHOULD'VE, he was calling all the students on the spaceship.

When I was back, I was told that we were surrounded with electromagnetic repulses, which were very dangerous for our machinery! I knew Rodrick should've got a solution for this thingy, as he is an expert in robotics!

"Hey... huff... how are ya... puff..." I said to Rodrick when I was at his mansion.

"NOT fine."

I saw Beatrice looking very serious at this situation.

"What's going on?" I asked.

"Electromagnetic trouble." Beatrice said.

I got towards them to see what they were doing. They were studying HISTORY!

"What idiotism!" I shouted "Why ye studying history in such a time, and I can see you got history books of all planets, with the same year opened- 2022!" I shouted.

"We are studying something IMPORTANT!" shouted Rodrick "In the month of January 2022, every book mentions that the inhabitants recorded a wave of headache and electromagnetic repulses, which means the cause is..."

"The Calsuset solar system's planets were lining-up thousand years ago!" I shouted.

That meant the planets produce electromagnetic repulses while lining-up!

Now almost everything was starting to explode! We had to do something, ANYTHING.

"Again, we are stuck between mess, so—" I was cut off.

"We'll do something, ANYTHING!" Rodrick shouted.

We got outta our mansions to see the problem, I got a device which tell about the electromagnetic repulses. When I was calculating the electromagnetic repulses, a WAVE of headache hit me.

"AAAAA..." I screamed.

"AAAAAA..." Beatrice screamed.

"AAAAAAAA..." Rodrick screamed.

"AAAAAAAAA..." we heard screams of peoples.

EVERYONE was screaming because of the headaches, when I found something.

"Guys, come here." I whispered.

I showed them that the useless thing we'd built for the 'advance eco-system' thingy was producing a different kind of wave which was multiplying the electromagnetic repulses!

I quickly tried to reduce the effect, but it was all useless.

We gathered all the brain-stuff we had and made a plan-

1. Try to STOP the advance eco-system device thingy.

Ok, it isn't a very cool plan, just one step, but we gone with it.

I climbed up till its power source, the only thing which did what it was supposed to do.

I jumbled some wires brainlessly, to end up with a black face (the circuit exploded). But it was a 'Nanocrystal battery' which could be charged for 9999... years! The thing I did just boosted the battery! Everything was going wrong; every single device was exploded!

Okay, some powerful devices were left, but they were also useless as their power sources were exploded.

We tried to make another plan-

1. Gather all people on the ship.
2. Help Vincent to get to the ship's cockpit.
3. Escape electromagnetic fields!

We gathered everyone in the school's hall and told them our plan.

"HURRAAAAAAAAAAAY!" everyone shouted.

We were excited for the plan, and I had the feeling for the first time that I could be friends with an inhabitant of a faraway galaxy!

We were altogether a single team, trying to get to the cockpit.

In the way, all sorts of devices were victim of our hands, we ripped all the devices off!!!!!!

The ship was almost destroyed!!
We finally reached the cockpit.

"huff... puff... I can't fly the ship, my hand's broken. A mindless robot grabbed it before exploding, so sorry. Yeah! Erick will be the copilot and Beatrice will be the pilot!" Vincent said.

"Yes sir, I'll be the pilot!" Beatrice shouted with enthusiasm in her voice.

I don't know how, but I agreed!

Before we could start the ship, something exploded, and I fell off on a planet along with Beatrice and some other kids!!

"What the heck?" Beatrice shouted.

"Good that we can still brea—" I was gonna say 'Good that we can still breath', when I started suffocating due to the loss of oxygen.

I quickly scanned my backpack for some mini-oxygen tanks.

I gave it to everyone who *needed* oxygen.

We looked at the ship and decided to get inside.

"As the gravity is less, we can use the extra oxygen tank for some boost and jump till the ship." I suggested.

Everyone was onboard with my plan!

I did all the things as decided, till we were just about an INCH away from our ship. Then, we fell with a crash.

"sorry..."

We tried more foolish plans until all the students and teachers landed on the same planet.

"We were trying to rescue you while we also fell down." Principle steward said.

We again made a better plan, with some better materials.

We got a zero-g device, which disables gravity in a particular area.

We again repeated my original plan, but with zero gravity this time, and we succeeded!

We entered from the back of the ship, sneaking like thieves in our OWN ship.

When we were back, I heard a volcano erupt, which almost caused my skin to run off my body!

To my bad luck, a volcano eruption had caused a HUGE hole in the ship. I fell in that hole and was falling towards a pool of LAVA!!

Then, I saw an alien... no, it must be an angel...

diving in the hole to save me, risking his own LIFE.

He dived to catch me, opened a pair of wings and flew back to the ship.

"Th- Than- Thanks!" I said with tears in my life.

"Your welcome! And you can call me Noah." The alien, Noah said.

"I'm Erick, Erick Woods!" I said.

We were again at the back of the ship, with only one way to the cockpit, the drainage system.

I filled my lungs with air and tried not to breath in there, but I immediately had to breath, and I *really* barfed!

When I was a little comfortable, I tried moving forward.

After an eternity, we reached a place where the pipe got a very small, only my bottomless bag could fit, I couldn't.

The pipe seemed to block everyone's path. everyone's, except Noah's, who could be as small as he wished!

"I have an idea!" Beatrice shouted to get everyone's attention. "Noah can be small, and we cannot, so we'll use Erick's bottomless bag, which can easily go-through the pipe! We'll sit in the bag and Noah will get us through!"

All of us quickly got inside, and we all were placed in shelves of our sizes.

"Incredible!!" Beatrice whispered to me.

I could see all my forgotten things and memories inside, all placed in their shelves.

I could see my first hoverboard, my favorite childhood toys, books, holo-pens, bikes and photo albums! Those memories bought TEARS to my eyes.

We waited till Noah asked us to come out, to see the cockpit.

We piloted the ship to drop all the students at their home-planets and the final stop was Earth.

"Wow, the blue planet." Rodrick said.

We all were all happy to see our good ol' Earth.

"Students get to your *real* houses, wherever they are. We are gonna replace the ship with a new one, till that time, you'll be going to the Earth school." Steward said.

I said goodbye to my friends and got home to surprise my parents that I was back.

The End

Things That You May Like To Understand More About-

1. *Mineralals*- They were found around the year 2067. They have a very funny story-

Once, some people were mining for coal, and found a mineralal named 'coalzite'. (coalzite is a better version of coal). They sold all the coalzite and made some money, but a buyer said the coal (coalzite) was an explosive; when he used it in his fireplace, it **EXPLODED**. There were more cases like this. There was an investigation which proved that the coalzite was not coal and was found deeper than coal. Many more mineralals were found. The definition of mineralal is 'A better mineral or energy source'.

1. Nebula

like states make a country, intelligent planets and galaxies make a nebula (the term was created in the year 3022).

3. Do you ever wonder what did the elder students do while I, Beatrice and Rodrick were protecting the ship from the invading bright-purple aliens?

No, they weren't on the field trip. Our school isn't that cheap, we have a whole ship for each grade!!!

About The Author-

Erick woods, he is a very intelligent and brilliant kid who had a dream to go study in outer space. His wish was fulfilled on 13th October, 3021.

His hobbies are-

Galactic Football, baseball, designing robots, programming robots, reading, writing, mathematics, etc.

About The Real Author-

Varad Kale, I am 12 years old and study in 6th grade. I am very much fond of reading. One day I thought, "Why not write a book?" and here it is, the sequel of my first book. I thought many times before writing each word of this book, to make it amazing!

My hobbies are studying Science, Math, Quantum Physics (learning it), reading storybooks and encyclopedias, vlogging, participating in Olympiads, eating (Pizza and Paneer), playing Kabaddi etc.

I promise there'll be another sequel to this series, in fact it is almost completed!

I hope you liked the book and look forward for your review.

www.ingramcontent.com/pod-product-compliance
Lightning Source LLC
Chambersburg PA
CBHW031004180726
47993CB00018B/1554